Crazy Love

by

Eric Brown

First published in 2006 in Great Britain by
Barrington Stoke Ltd
www.barringtonstoke.co.uk

Copyright © 2006 Eric Brown

The moral right of the author has been asserted in
accordance with the Copyright, Designs and
Patents Act 1988

ISBN-10: 1-84299-367-4
ISBN-13:   978-1-84299-367-5

Printed in Great Britain by Bell & Bain Ltd

A Note from the Author

I had the idea for this book when I was at the zoo. I was watching a group of school-children, and one girl said to her friend, "Bet you wouldn't go out with ..."

A few days later my editor at Barrington Stoke asked me if I'd like to write a love story. I said yes, and began to think about what the story might be.

And then I remembered what I'd heard at the zoo. I put my writing cap on – that's like a thinking cap, only bigger. I thought *Did the girl at the zoo ever go out with the class dork?* Maybe she did, and maybe they fell in love and maybe their story had a happy ending ...

To John McDermott,
Jackie Tyler
and Kate

Contents

Hi, I'm Trish – Trish Green.

This is my diary. I kept it for a week. It was the most important week of my life.

I didn't like myself before that week. I was a bitch, a real bitch.

Then I met someone, and things began to get a lot better.

And then things got a lot worse ...

****

Chapter 1
Thursday

At the Zoo

I was on a school trip to the zoo with my friends Kate and Lisa. We were sitting next to the monkey cage and eating burgers. The rest of my class were with Mr Carter. They'd gone to have a good stare at the animals in the cages.

I wanted to stare at some animals, too. These animals were called *boys*.

There was another school at the zoo – the sixth-formers from a posh boys' school out in the country. Those lads were real cool. They were like some sexy boy band.

They'd seen us looking at them. Now they'd started to mess around and pretend to fight among themselves.

I was wearing my school uniform. I wished I was wearing my short denim skirt with the tight T-shirt that said **This Bitch Bites** on the front. Then the boys would *really* have stared at me.

I mean, I'm the best looking girl in my class. Everyone knows it. That's why Kate and Lisa hang around with me. They're both a bit fat, with round faces like burger buns.

"Put your tongue back in your mouth, Trish," Lisa said to me.

"They're looking at us!" Kate said.

I said, "Wrong. They're looking at *me*."

Lisa and Kate didn't say anything. They knew I was right.

The teacher in charge of the other school shouted at the boys. One of the boys smiled and waved at me, but I pretended I hadn't seen him. They followed the teacher to the car park and onto a coach.

Just my luck!

Kate said, "Cheer up, Trish. What about the lads in our year?"

"A bunch of dorks and losers," I told her.

"Even Gaz?" Lisa asked.

"Well, maybe not Gaz," I said. I was kind of going out with Gaz. He was hard, a bit of a bully. He thought he was really big, one of the cool guys in the year. He wasn't in our science group so he hadn't come to the zoo with us.

"What about Denis?" Kate asked with a laugh.

I pulled a face as if I was going to be sick. "Denis? You mean, Denis dork Dobson?"

Denis was the last boy in class I'd ever go out with. Denis was a loser and a wimp. He had no friends – well, sometimes he went around with Fat Harry. Maybe he had one friend.

Kate gave me a nudge. "There he is. What a weirdo!"

Denis was sitting in front of the elephant house. He was drawing something on the sketch-pad he always took round with him. He was concentrating really hard. The tip of his tongue was poking out of his mouth.

It was really odd, but I hated Denis then. I don't know why. Perhaps because he wasn't like the sexy lads that had just left the zoo.

I wanted to hurt him. I mean, really hurt him. Inside. Not like punch him or anything. But show him up. Make him feel small.

Is that cruel, or what? That's me. Like my mum says – I can be an angel one minute and an evil bitch the next.

I was bored. I didn't want to be at the zoo. I'd rather have gone shopping. Perhaps it was because I was bored and hated the zoo that I said to Lisa and Kate, "Hey, listen. I'm gonna have some fun with Dork Dobson."

Kate and Lisa looked at me. "Like what?" Lisa asked.

"Just watch me," I said. I got up and walked over to where Denis was sitting in front of the elephant house.

He saw me coming. I put on a sexy walk. I even smiled at him and licked my lips. He looked like a frightened rabbit!

"Hiya, Denis," I said.

He nodded. "Hi, Trish," he said. He looked back at the drawing he was doing. It was an elephant's head. He was turning bright red.

A drop of sweat ran down his cheek.

"What you doing, Denis?" I said.

"Drawing," he whispered.

"What you drawing, Denis?" I said.

He gave me a quick look. I could see he was scared and that was what I wanted. "An elephant," he said. "The bull. It's 40 years old. The sign says it's the oldest elephant in England. It's called Maliki. That's Swahili for King."

I said, very sweetly, "Denis, I really don't give a shit what Maliki means." I stopped, and then said, "I came here to talk to you."

He swallowed. His hand was shaking. "Me?" he said in a small voice.

I just smiled at him, my best smile. My mates say that when I smile like that I look just like Britney Spears. Older than 15, and dead sexy.

So I sat down right next to Denis. I made sure that our legs were touching.

He went very still. He didn't move at all. *What's it like to be him*, I thought, *with me sitting next to him.* I pressed my long brown legs against his trousers. I bet his heart was beating so fast he could hardly breathe!

"Denis," I said.

He didn't say anything for a long time. Then he said, "What?"

I got hold of the bubble gum I was chewing and pulled it out of my mouth. I rolled the gum into a ball and said, "Want to share it?"

He shook his head. "No, thanks."

I looked disappointed. "Oh, some lads think it's *sexy* to share gum."

He shook his head again. "Not me."

I laughed and said, "You got a girlfriend, Denis?"

He took a deep breath. He tried to go back to his drawing, but his hand was shaking so much that he made a mess of the elephant's trunk.

"Well, *do* you have a girlfriend?" I asked again.

"No."

"What, a big lad like you? I thought you'd have a load of girls waiting to go out with you."

I looked back at Lisa and Kate. They were sitting close together now and hugging each other, laughing.

I said, "How would you like to go out with Kate or Lisa?"

He shook his head, not looking at me. "No thanks."

"No," I said. "Don't blame you. I mean, they're dogs, yeah?"

He just shrugged.

I went on, "And anyway, they don't want to go out with you."

"Good," he said, rubbing out the elephant's trunk. Then he began to draw it again.

I don't know what made me say it, but I went, "I know someone who does want to go out with you, Denis."

He was silent. He was sweating even more now. He didn't know where to look.

I said, "Do you know who wants to go out with you, Denis?"

He shrugged. "How should I know?"

I smiled at him and said, "Look at me."

He turned his head and looked at me. I said, "I really want to go out with you, Denis."

I mean, weird or what? I didn't know I was going to say that. It just came out. I knew it was the best way to hurt him.

His voice was shaking. "You?" he said.

"Yeah, me. You up for it? How about tonight? Meet you outside Jackson's in town at eight, OK? We'll go to the park, mess around, yeah?"

I didn't wait for him to answer. I just stood up and walked away. I bet he was watching my bum, undressing me in his dirty little head.

I got back to Kate and Lisa and dragged them around the back of the elephant house. I told them what I'd said and we wet ourselves laughing.

Chapter 2
Thursday Night

"Stuck Up Bitch"

I wasn't going to meet Denis, of course.

I'd stay at home and think about him hanging around outside Jackson's. He wouldn't know where I was. He'd be so upset when I didn't turn up.

As if a girl like me would really go out with a loser like Denis!

I looked at myself in the bedroom mirror and said, "It's all about power, girl!"

I was wearing my white Levi's jeans and a tight top. The top had the words: **No Car? No Money? No Chance!** going right across my chest.

Gaz rang me on his mobile. He said he was going out with some mates. He wouldn't see me tonight.

So I said, "That's fine. You can piss off then."

"Trish," he said, "don't say that."

"It's over between us, Gaz. Find someone else to mess around, OK?"

"You can't do this!" he said.

"Oh, can't I?" I said. And I turned off my mobile so he couldn't call me back.

I looked at myself in the mirror and gave myself a sly smile. What was Gaz going to say to me at school in the morning. He'd be like, "Please, Trish. I'm sorry, OK? I really love you, you know? Let's try again."

And I'd be like, "Gaz, go drown yourself in a pool of piss. It's over. Finished. End of story."

That'd teach him to go off with his mates like that.

I looked at my old Mickey Mouse clock. It was seven-thirty.

I was bored and had nothing to do and I had a sudden mad idea ...

I said to myself, "Have some more fun with Denis the Dork! Frighten him to death!"

So I ran from the house, caught the bus into town and hurried across the street to Jackson's.

****

I was early. It was five to eight, so I went into a paper shop and looked at the magazines. I was near the window so I could look out for Denis coming.

The town hall clock was striking eight when I saw him. Right on time. He walked towards Jackson's and sat down outside on a bench.

It was odd. He looked different. He wasn't wearing his school uniform. He looked smart. He had new jeans and a white Gap T-shirt, and his hair was gelled. I mean, he didn't look bad, for a dork.

I was going to go out and have some more fun – but then I saw something.

Kate and Lisa were across the street. They were over in the doorway of Next. They were hidden so no one could see them and they were giggling like five-year-olds.

OK, so I had told them about meeting Denis – I'd told them what I'd said to Denis at the zoo. But I didn't think they'd turn up to watch! After all, as far as they knew, I wasn't going to be there.

Well, I'd give them something to talk about at school tomorrow. I'd frighten Denis so much that Kate and Lisa would laugh themselves stupid!

Only, it didn't happen like that.

I was about to leave the paper shop and go over to Denis, when Kate and Lisa ran across the street and started talking to him.

I wanted to go up to them and ask what they were playing at. This was my party and they were spoiling it.

They talked for about two minutes, and then Denis shrugged and walked away. Kate and Lisa just stared at him.

Lisa pulled her mobile out of her pocket and began to punch in some numbers.

Guess what?

My mobile went off. "Yeah?" I said.

Lisa said, "Trish? You at home?"

I said, "What if I am?"

I watched them through the window. They were right up close together so both of them could hear me. Lisa said, "Only ... guess where we are, Trish?"

"Let me think? Mars? The moon?"

"Wrong. In town, in front of Jackson's."

"So?" I said.

"So," Lisa said, "we've just seen Dobson."

"Great. So what?"

Lisa said, all excited, "So ... you thought he'd be annoyed, yeah? That you didn't turn up. You thought he really wanted to meet you?"

"Maybe."

"Wrong. He knew you were kidding. He said he didn't want to meet you anyway, said he didn't like you—"

I stared through the window. Kate grabbed the phone. She said, "Do you know what Denis *really* said?"

"Go on ..." I said.

"He said you were a stuck up bitch who loved herself. He said you were a slut—"

I felt myself going red. Anger boiled up in me. I thought I was going to explode.

Kate said, "Dobson said you were best off going out with a brain-dead moron like Gaz."

I turned off my phone and looked through the window. Lisa and Kate stared at each other, then they burst out laughing. They walked away, and I just stood there. What could I do next?

Then I knew exactly what I was going to do.

I walked out of the paper shop and turned right. I was running after Denis. He'd be going back to the station, that's where his bus stop was, for the bus back to his village.

I was angry. I wanted to do something bad to Denis the Dork Dobson, something he'd never forget ...

Then I saw him. He was standing outside WH Smith's, looking at a pile of sketch pads in the window.

I ran up to him.

****

Life's weird, isn't it?

Sometimes I find myself doing things without really thinking. They just happen, as if somebody in my head is making me say and do these things ...

Denis turned and stared at me.

And I found myself saying, "Denis! Sorry I was late! Missed the bus ..."

He just stared at me. He said, "I've just seen Kate and Lisa."

I shrugged. "So?"

"So, they told me that you didn't really want to go out with me."

I laughed. "They were lying! They're jealous, yeah? Of course I want to go out with you. I mean, I'm here, aren't I?"

That made him think.

I smiled my best smile. "So," I said, "where are we going?"

21

"Do you mean it? Do you really want to go out with me?"

I did something I didn't mean to do. I reached out and held his hand. "Let's go and buy a burger," I said, "and then we'll go for a walk in the park."

Chapter 3
Ducks and Dorks

We went to Burger King and Denis said he'd pay. So I ordered a double cheese burger with fries and a milkshake.

We walked to the park. Denis was so nervous he didn't know what to say. He kept looking at me and smiling. What a geek!

I didn't know what I was going to do to hurt him. But he'd said those things about me – he said I was a stuck up bitch and a slut. I'd make him pay for that.

But now I was all smiles and wide eyes and chatty with him. Later, I'd make him sorry.

I did most of the talking – I'm good like that. Mum said that if talking was an Olympic sport, I'd win a gold medal.

"Where did you live before coming here?" I asked.

He shrugged. "Bradford. Then Dad got a new job here so we had to move."

"Do you like it here?"

"It's OK, I suppose."

"You don't have many friends, do you?" I said. We walked along by the pond.

He went red and shrugged again. "It's hard when you're new," he said.

He was watching some ducks on the pond. "Let's sit down," he said.

So we sat on a bench. Denis stared at the ducks swimming in the water.

And guess what he did then?

I couldn't believe it. He pulled a small note-book from the back pocket of his jeans and began drawing in it with a little pencil.

I said, "What are you doing?"

"Sorry. I take this everywhere I go."

"Hello," I said, "they're, like, just *ducks*!"

He glanced at me. "They're not *just* ducks," he said. "They've come here all the way from Siberia. They're Golden-eyes."

I nodded. "Golden-eye ducks," I said. "Great."

I looked at the drawing he was doing of the ducks on the water. I had to admit that it was good.

I said, "You like animals, don't you?"

He nodded. He didn't look up but went on drawing the ducks. "I like animals and drawing," he said.

"So what do you want to be when you leave school?" I asked him. "An animal artist?"

"An illustrator," he said. "Books, magazines. I'd like to draw animals, but I can draw anything really." He stopped drawing and looked at me. "What about you? What do you want to do?"

I shrugged. "Dunno. Never really thought about it. Get married to someone rich and have tons of kids, I suppose. I want to be looked after. Spend lots of time buying new clothes and make-up and stuff."

He looked at me. "Don't you want a real job?"

"You mean, work like my mum five days a week and come home tired and grumpy? No way!"

"You could get a job you really liked."

"Don't see the point. My husband can work. I'll look after my kids."

He laughed and said, "That's hard work too, you know."

I said, "Beats working in a factory."

"Is that what your dad does?"

"Nah. Dad left home when I was five. Haven't seen him since. Don't know what he does."

Denis shut the note-book and slipped it back into his pocket. He was silent. Then he said, "I thought you were going out with Gaz?"

I laughed. "No way. He'd rather spend time with his mates, so I dumped him."

Denis nodded. He said, "So ... why did you go out with him in the first place?"

"'Cos he's fit and cute and he said he liked me. But, like, once he got what he wanted, he started pissing around with his mates again ..."

I looked at Denis. He was going red.

I said, "So ... why do you think I wanted to go out with you?"

He was bright red by now, and sweating again. He shrugged and mumbled something. It sounded like, "Dunno."

I said, "'Cos you're different. You don't say much. And ... you know something, you look good in jeans and that T-shirt."

As if!

Denis looked awkward. He shuffled on the bench and looked at his watch. "Last bus is at nine-thirty. I've got to be home by ten. School tomorrow and all that ..."

I tried not to laugh. What a mummy's boy!

I said, "I catch the same bus, Den. I don't live far from you."

We walked to the bus stop and waited for the number 35 bus. I just hoped that no one from school saw me with Denis the Dork.

We got on the bus and sat on the top deck, right at the front. I held his hand. He went stiff. His hand was red hot.

I felt ... kind of powerful. I was in control. I was sexy and good-looking and Denis was scared to death of me.

The bus left town and moved down the narrow country lanes. Denis stared through the window, not looking at me.

Two minutes later I said, "This is my stop." I turned to him. "Well, aren't you going to give me a kiss?"

He just looked at me as if I'd asked him to rob a bank. Horrified.

"Hey, you never kissed a girl before?"

I leaned forward. I didn't really want to kiss the Dork – but I did want to frighten him.

He said, "Hey, I'll get off here with you! I want to show you something."

And before I could say anything, he jumped up and ran down the stairs. I got up and followed him.

****

We stood in the lane as the bus roared away.

It was still light. The sun was setting and the sky was red.

Denis pointed to some trees next to the lane.

"What?" I said.

"I come here every few days," Denis said. "A few weeks ago, I found something."

I gave him my best 'oh yeah' look. "Like what?" I said.

"I was walking through the woods and I saw this bird. A red kite. There's not many in this area. I saw it fly into a big oak tree. So I went and had a look and found a nest with three eggs in it."

Yeah, great! What kind of loser was Denis the Dork, anyway? It's late at night, and Denis is standing in the lane and trying to impress me with a story about a red kite and its eggs! Get a life!

"Come on," he said. "I'll show you."

I wanted to walk away, go home. But something stopped me. "OK," I said. I followed him into the trees.

We pushed through grass and stuff. The ground was wet. My new shoes were going to be wrecked! We came to a path and Denis led the way to a big tree.

"Up there," he said, and he pointed into the branches.

I looked up. I could see a dark blob of twigs high up in the branches.

"That's really, really something," I said. "I mean, that's really great. A bird's nest!"

Denis was pulling something from a bush next to the tree. I watched him. I couldn't believe it. He was dragging a ladder from the bush, then he put it up against the oak tree.

"Are you mad or what?" I said.

He just grinned at me.

Then he climbed up the ladder and peered into the bird's nest. "Three eggs!" he called down to me. "They're beautiful!"

He climbed down again and stood beside me. "Go on. Go and have a look."

I stared at him, and then at the ladder, and then all the way up to the bird's nest high up in the tree. "Do you know something, Denis? I think I'd rather stay down here. I'm sure you understand."

He shrugged and pulled down the ladder and hid it in the bushes again.

We made our way back to the lane.

I pointed at some houses down the lane. "I live there, Den. Thanks for a ... a great night," I said.

Yeah, like looking at ducks on the pond and staring up at a bird's nest, I thought.

33

He lifted his hand and waved, but didn't try to kiss me. "Can ... I mean, can I see you again, Trish?"

I smiled. "Maybe. I'll think about it."

I wanted to ask him why he'd called me a bitch and a slut, but now wasn't the time.

I waved, "Bye, Den." I turned and walked home.

On the way, I thought about what he'd said about me, and how I could hurt him. No one called me things and got away with it!

Chapter 4
Friday

The Nest

Next day at first break Kate came running up to me. "Is it true?" she asked.

I said, "Is what true?"

"You and Denis Dobson. Are you really seeing him?"

I stared at her. "As if! Who told you that?"

Kate said, "Lisa saw you in the park last night. She says you were holding hands. Holding hands with Denis the Dork! Were you?"

"Get real," I said. "Lisa's lying. Do you think I'd really go with the Dork?"

Kate ran off. Two minutes later she came back, and she was dragging Lisa with her. Lisa stared at me, and I stared back at her. We were like two boxers before a fight.

"Well?" I said.

Kate said, "What did you see, Lisa?"

"I was in the park," Lisa said. "You and Dobson were sitting by the pond. You were holding his hand and staring into his eyes all lovey-dovey." She put her fingers into her mouth. "Retch time!" Lisa said.

"Piss off, Lisa. You're lying," I hissed.

"Trish and Dobson – true love!" Lisa said with a laugh and she walked away.

Kate stared at me. "Well?" she said. "Are you and Dobson ... you know ...?"

"What do you think?" I said. "I could have my pick of any lad in school. Why should I go with the Dork?"

"But Lisa saw you!"

Then it came to me. An idea.

"Listen," I said in a whisper, "I'll let you into a secret, but don't tell anyone, OK?"

Kate nodded. "OK. Promise."

"I was with Dobson last night, but it wasn't what you think," I said. "You know what he said about me, how he called me a bitch and stuff, yeah? Well, I want to get even with him, yeah? I want to hurt him."

Kate stared at me. "How?" she asked.

I smiled. "He showed me something last night ..."

I told Kate all about the red kite's nest in the big oak tree, and what I planned to do that night.

****

On the bus home after school, Denis came and sat next to me. I looked around, but there was no one from school on the bus. "Hi, Den," I said sweetly.

"Trish, I was thinking ... Are you doing anything tonight? I mean, we could go and see a movie."

I made a disappointed face. "Den, I'm sorry. My mum's going out and I've got to look after my little sister, OK?" I was a good liar. I didn't want to see Denis again.

He nodded. "OK. But what about Saturday? You doing anything then?"

"I don't think so. Tell you what, give me your mobile number and I'll call you."

Denis shrugged. "I don't have a mobile," he said.

What a loser!

"Okay," I said. "What about your home number?"

So he gave me his home number and I said I'd ring him tomorrow.

I got home and made myself some beans on toast and watched TV. When Mum got in I told her I was going out.

Mum stared at me. "What, in scruffy jeans and a T-shirt? What's happened to my fashion model daughter?"

I shrugged. "Just going round to some friends," I lied.

I got out of the house and ran down the lane. At the bus stop I found the path into the trees.

My heart was beating fast. I wanted to hurt Denis, but I didn't want to get caught. What would happen if someone saw me?

I came to the big oak tree. The nest was a long way up.

I pulled the ladder from where Denis had hidden it in the bush. It was heavy – Denis must be stronger than he looked. I dragged the ladder to the tree and put it up against the tree trunk. Then I had a long rest. I was breathing hard and I felt hot and tired.

I looked up. The nest seemed even farther away, now.

"You've got to do it, girl," I told myself.

So I climbed up, step by step. I didn't look down. If I looked down, I'd wet myself with fright.

I pushed the branches to one side. The nest was just there. I took another step up and looked into the nest and saw three big, white eggs.

All I had to do now was reach out and grab the eggs. Then I'd drop them to the ground. I could pull the nest out of the branches too and drop that after the eggs.

I thought of Denis the Dork's face when he came to check on his little secret ...

I put my hand out for the eggs, then stopped.

I thought about it. The eggs had baby chicks in them. If I dropped the eggs, I'd be hurting Denis, but I'd also be killing the chicks.

I know I'm a bitch, but how could I do a thing like that? How could I do that just to get back at Denis for calling me names?

So I left the nest alone. I climbed back down the ladder and put it back in the bushes. And do you know what? When I left the woods and walked home, I felt good that I hadn't wrecked the red kite's nest.

Chapter 5
Saturday

First Impressions

I didn't ring Denis. But he rang me.

"Yeah, who is it?" I said.

It was Denis. "I got your number from Kate," he said. "I hope you don't mind me ringing you."

"That's OK," I said.

"Only ... are you doing anything tonight? Would you like to go to a movie?"

I could see Denis tonight. Then I'd dump him and tell him that it was a big mistake. I'd tell him that I wanted more from a boyfriend than ducks and red kites.

"Yeah, OK."

He said, "And I've got you something. A present. See you outside Jackson's at seven, okay?"

I got ready, then caught the bus into town. I wondered what the present was. Earrings, a ring – something expensive? But what would Denis the Dork know about buying a present for a girl?

I bet he'd bought me a book about birds!

When I got to town he was sitting on the bench outside Jackson's again.

"Hi, Trish."

"Hi, Den," I said.

He held my hand. And do you know something? It felt OK. I mean, me and Denis the Dork, holding hands!

What was happening to me?

I told myself that after the movie, when he'd paid for my ticket and bought me a Coke, I'd dump him ...

We walked across town and went into the cinema. We sat at the back and watched the new Harry Potter movie. Den didn't try anything. He just held my hand. Gaz would have been all over me – trying to get his hand into my knickers.

Half-way through the film, I started to think about what Den might have got me. He said he'd bought me a present, but he wasn't carrying anything.

We went to the cinema café after the film and Den bought me a coffee.

Then he pulled something from under his shirt. It was a big brown envelope. He passed it to me.

"What is it?" I said.

"Open it and see," he told me.

I opened the envelope and looked inside. There was a piece of card inside the envelope. I pulled it out. Stuck onto the card was a drawing on white paper.

I stared at the drawing. It was me – but different.

"What do you think?" Den asked.

I looked at him. "It's amazing. It looks … beautiful. You drew this?"

He nodded.

"It's great," I said. "But the clothes … You've drawn me in old clothes – ragged jeans and a torn T-shirt."

He shrugged. "Trish, it doesn't matter what you wear. You don't need designer labels to look good. What matters is what you're like in here." He touched his chest. "People are more bothered about the sort of person you are than the clothes you wear. Honest."

I looked at him. "But the first thing people see is your clothes," I said. "You've got to look good. Make an impression."

He shook his head. "Clothes might be the first thing people see. But after that they see the person inside them." He looked at me. "Think about Gaz, for instance."

"What about him?"

"What did you think about him when you first saw him?"

I shrugged. "He was good looking, wore smart clothes, had nice hair ..."

Den said, "And then you got to know him, and what did you think then?"

I smiled. "I thought he was a right big-head who didn't give a shit about anyone but himself."

Den was smiling at me. "So ... you see. First impressions don't matter that much."

I thought about that and shrugged. "Maybe you're right," I said. "But I'm not going to start wearing old rags!"

Den smiled and asked me if I wanted another coffee. He went to get it. When he came back with two cups, he said, "What did you think about me when you first saw me?"

I looked away. *Should I tell him the truth?* I thought. What I said was, "I thought you could do with some new clothes, and a hair cut. And you weren't into anything that the other lads were into, like football and music. You liked animals and birds and drawing ..."

"You thought I was a loser, right?"

I looked away. "Well ... I thought you were *odd*."

He took a sip of his coffee and said, "And what do you think now?"

I laughed. "Still think you're odd!" I said. I looked away. I didn't feel right. I wanted to talk about something else.

So I said, "What did you think about the film?"

We talked about the Harry Potter film for a while. Den said that he'd got all the books and read them too. He told me all about them. I was amazed at how much he could remember, and how he made it all sound so interesting when he talked.

We caught the last bus home and sat on the top deck.

I thought about what I had planned earlier. I'd planned to dump Den, to tell him that I didn't want to see him again.

But ... something inside me wouldn't let me say the words.

When the bus came to my stop, I kissed him quickly on the lips. "Thanks for the drawing!" I said. I ran down the stairs and jumped off the bus.

When I got home I sat on my bed for a long time and stared at the drawing of me that Den had done. It was great. I looked fantastic – even if I was wearing old clothes.

He must have taken a long time to draw something so good.

I pinned it on the wall by my bed. Then I closed my eyes and tried to sleep. I thought about everything Den had said that night.

Chapter 6
Monday

The Fight

On Monday before assembly, Kate came up to me and said, "Is it true, Trish? Are you really going out with Denis?"

"Who said I am?"

She grabbed my arm. "Is it true?" she said.

"What if it is?"

She just stared at me. Her mouth hung open and her eyes were massive. "You are! You're really going out with Denis the Dork!"

I pushed her arm away. "We're just friends," I said. "And anyway, he isn't a dork."

Kate stared at me. "Listen to you! Last week you thought he was minging!"

I shrugged. "Things change," I said. "You get to know people ..."

Kate ran off and grabbed Lisa. "Guess what?" I heard her say. "Trish is seeing Dobson!"

I looked for Denis in assembly, but I couldn't find him.

At lunch break I was eating my sandwiches outside. Gaz walked across the yard and stood over me. "Hi, Trish."

"Gaz," I said.

"Look, the other day. Sorry about that. I had to see these mates."

I gave him my sweetest smile. "That's okay."

He grinned at me. "It's okay? You mean that? You mean, you'll see me again? We could go out tonight."

"I don't think so, Gaz," I said.

He looked like I'd punched him in the gut. "Why not? I said I'm sorry."

"Like I said on the phone, Gaz. It's over. You and me are history. I don't want to see you again. I don't even want to talk to you, thank you very much."

He went red with anger. "It's true then," he said under his breath.

I sipped my juice through the straw, then said, "What is?"

"You're going out with that arsehole, Dobson."

"What's it got to do with you if I am?"

He shook his head. "I don't believe it. Trish and Dobson ... Wait till I see him!"

I pushed my face close to his. "If you lay a finger on Den ..." I began.

He just looked at me the way he does when you can see how great he thinks he is. "Yeah, what will you do, Trish?" he said. "Will you beat me up? Oh, I am frightened."

I stood up and stared at him. "You know something, Gaz? You think you're so great. Mr Big Man. I'll tell you this – Den is so much nicer than you'll ever be!"

That did it. Gaz exploded. He grabbed my arm so fast that my drink went flying.

"You cow!" he said. Then he dragged me behind the bike-shed and pushed me against the wall. I was shaking. I knew that he was about to hit me.

He put his face so close to mine that I could smell his breath. He said, "Dobson is a piece of shit. How can you go with a faggot like him?"

"He's a good person," I said. "He's kind and—"

Gaz grabbed my arm again and squeezed. I cried out in pain. "Stop it!" I yelled.

"Dump him!" Gaz said. "I'll give you one last chance – dump Dobson and go out with me!"

"As if I'd go out with an ape like you!" I spat.

Then he hit me. I wasn't expecting it. I was shocked when his hand smacked me across the face. My cheek was stinging and tears came to my eyes.

"You bastard!" I yelled.

He was about to hit me again, but a voice said, "Leave her alone!"

I turned. It was Den.

It was odd. It was great to see him then, but at the same time I didn't want Gaz to beat him up.

Gaz just looked at Den and sneered, "What did you say?"

Den smiled at me. Then he turned back to Gaz and said, "I said, leave her alone."

Gaz laughed. "Or else? What will you do?"

Den stepped forward.

I said, "Don't, Den. Go away. He'll beat you up. I don't want you to get hurt."

Den said, "Only thugs pick on girls. Why don't you hit me, if you're so tough?"

Gaz smiled. I could see the look of cruelty on his face. It was horrible.

Then Gaz grabbed Den's shirt, and with his other hand he punched Den in the face. He came at him so fast and hard that Den didn't stand a chance. He groaned and fell to his knees. I screamed. Blood poured out of Den's nose.

Gaz hit him again, and again. Den was still on his knees, staring up as Gaz punched him in the face. "This'll teach you, Dobson!" Gaz shouted at him. "If you go near Trish again, I'll kill you!"

I jumped at Gaz. I tried to hit him, but he just elbowed me in the face. I screamed and held my cheek.

Seconds later it was all over. I heard a shout and turned around. Mr Carter was running across the yard. He pulled Gaz away from Den. "You little thug!" Carter said. "In my office, now!" He held Gaz by the neck, and

Gaz just sneered at me as Carter led him away across the yard.

I helped Den to his feet and mopped the blood with a tissue.

I felt a lot of things then. I hated Gaz. And I felt terrible that Den had got beaten up so badly because of me.

But most of all I felt so proud of Den.

****

After school I said to Den, "Come over to my house. Mum doesn't get in till six. How does your nose feel?"

He touched his nose and top lip. "Sore. But I'll live."

I held his hand as we walked home. "You know something, Den? What you did, then, how you stuck up for me …"

"I couldn't just let him hit you like that!"

I looked at him. "Thank you."

When we got home I poured two glasses of Coke and carried them into the lounge.

We sat on the sofa.

"I want to ask you something," I said.

I was still thinking of how Den had told Kate and Lisa that I was a bitch and a slut. That still hurt. I wanted to know if he still thought I was those things.

I said, "That first night before we met, you said those things about me to Kate and Lisa."

He shook his head. "What things?"

"Outside Jackson's. When I was late meeting you. Kate told me you said I was a stuck up bitch and a slut."

He opened his mouth. I could see he was shocked. "I never! All I said was that I wasn't bothered about going out with you. I thought you'd stood me up, that was all."

"You didn't say those things about me? Honest truth?" I said.

"Honest," he said. "Kate's lying."

I nodded. That sounded like Kate …

He said, "You do believe me, don't you?"

I nodded. "'Course I do, Den," I said.

We just sat on the sofa and chatted for ages, and an odd thing happened. You know how it is when you're with a really cool guy, and all you can think about is kissing him and ripping his clothes off? Well, I began to feel hot, and all these ideas filled my head … about me and Den doing it on the sofa …

I'm glad I didn't try to rip his clothes off, because a minute later Mum came in. She stopped in the doorway when she saw us sitting on the sofa.

"Oh, and who is this?" Mum asked.

Denis stood up and smiled. "Denis. I'm a friend of Trish's," he said.

Mum smiled. "Nice to meet you, Denis."

Later, I told Den we'd meet after school tomorrow and go to the café in the park. I watched him walk down the lane. Then I went back into the lounge.

Mum said, "Well, Denis seems a nice lad, Trish."

I went up to my room and lay on my bed. My head was full of Den. I couldn't think about anything else.

Last week I thought Denis Dobson was the biggest dork in the world.

And now ...

Love is weird. Love is crazy.

Chapter 7
Tuesday

"You've Changed ..."

Next day at school I found Kate looking in my locker. I'd left it open first thing and forgotten to lock it. When I walked around the corner into the corridor, I saw Kate open the door of my locker and put her hand inside.

"Hey!" I yelled. "What do you think you're doing!"

She pulled her hand out. Her face was burning. "Oh, I thought ... I'm sorry! I made a mistake. I though this was Lisa's locker. She wanted—"

"Liar!" I said, and opened the door. Then I saw what she had done.

A bit of paper was stuck onto the inside of the door. On the paper were the words: Slut Trish 4 Dork Denis!

I tore the paper down and scrunched it into a ball.

Then I pushed it into Kate's face. I tried to stuff the paper into her fat mouth.

She ran off down the corridor and I just stood there. I'd never felt as angry in my life. I slammed the locker door shut, then locked it and went out into the yard.

I walked to the fence and stared across the street. Tears stung my eyes. Why were people so cruel?

"Are you OK?"

I turned around. It was Den. He was staring at me. He looked upset, as if he was worried about me. He reached out and took me in his arms, and it felt great. It felt like he really did care, and would protect me.

The bell went, and I swore. I wanted to stand with his arms around me all afternoon.

****

After school I met Den and we walked into the park and sat outside the café. We had some coffee. The sun was shining. I pointed at the ducks on the pond. "Golden-eyes," I said. "All the way from Siberia."

Den laughed.

We talked. It was amazing. He was interested in everything I said. I told him all about my mum and dad, how they had split

up. We talked about music, and the films
we'd seen. Then Den told me about the books
he liked. When he talked about them it was
as if they'd come alive for me.

And all the time my heart was beating so
fast I thought I would faint.

Later we went to Burger King, and this
time *I* bought *him* dinner.

He put his burger down and said, "You've
changed, Trish."

"Have I? How?"

He shrugged. "It's hard to say. When I
first met you ... I don't know. You seemed
hard. Mean."

"Are you trying to say that I was a bitch?"

"No!" he said quickly. He shrugged.
"Perhaps it was because I didn't really know
you. Now I do know you. I can see past all
the sexy clothes and make-up."

I smiled at him. "And what do you see?"

He laughed. "I see someone who wants to be loved," he said in a small voice.

We went to the cinema. I can't remember anything about the film. We just sat on the back row and started kissing, and we never stopped. We just held each other and kissed all the way through the film, until the lights came on.

We had to run like idiots to catch the last bus, and when we climbed onto the top deck we were at it again … kissing like we'd never see each other again.

That night I lay in bed and thought about Denis for hours and hours.

Chapter 8
Wednesday and Thursday

Gaz Again

For the next two days Den and I met in town after school. We talked and talked and talked. It was the happiest time in my life. I felt great. When Den and I were together, my heart felt like it was going to burst. When I wasn't with him, I felt as if something was wrong. All I could think about was Den. I was so in love with him that I felt sick when he wasn't holding me ...

On Thursday at school, the big news was that Kate and Gaz were going out.

I just laughed when Lisa told me. I said, "Kate and Gaz? They're just right for each other!"

I was glad that Gaz had found someone. Perhaps now he would stop being jealous about me and Den.

****

At break that afternoon, Gaz came up to me and said, "Still seeing the Dork?"

I gave him the evil eye. "You still seeing Fat Kate?" I sneered back.

"You're still the same bitch as ever, Trish."

"Then why did you go out with me?"

He laughed. "Why do you think?" he said. He shook his head. "And now you're doing it with the biggest dork in school—"

"And aren't you jealous?" I said. "You don't like it, do you? You don't like the idea that I dumped you and went out with Den."

He smiled, and I didn't like that smile. It was evil. "The other day, when I beat the living shit out of the Dork – that wasn't the end of it. Just the start," Gaz muttered.

"If you lay a finger on him," I began.

"Oh," Gaz said, all Mr Big again. "I'm not going to touch the Dork. I know how to hurt you. I know how to hurt *both* of you."

He didn't say another word. He just blew me a kiss and walked away.

Hurt both of us? I thought. I didn't like the sound of that one bit.

Chapter 9
Friday

The End

Den wasn't at school the next day. It was a Friday. I wanted to go somewhere special. We'd been seeing each other for more than a week.

After school I rang him at home. There was no answer.

I tried again. The phone just rang and rang and no one picked it up.

I felt so bad. I wanted to see Den so much that it hurt. I had to go round to his house, to see if he was there.

I knew where he lived. It was in a big house on the edge of the next village. I ran there from my house. My heart was thumping. Five minutes later I walked up the driveway to his house and rang the bell.

There was no reply.

I rang the bell again. "Come on, Den! Please!" I said to myself.

Then the door opened. A woman stood in the hall. She looked at me.

I smiled. "Hi. Is Denis in? I'm Trish."

The woman said, "I know who you are. Denis is in, but he doesn't want to see you. Goodbye." And she closed the door before I could say another word.

I just stared at the door with my mouth open.

Den didn't want to see me? But just last night we'd held each other and said how much we loved each other!

What had happened?

So I rang the bell again. I wanted to cry. I was in a panic. Why didn't Den want to see me?

I rang the bell again and again. This time the door opened so fast it gave me a fright. The same woman came to the door. She must have been Den's mum. "Don't you think you've hurt Denis enough, young lady!" she said, and she slammed the door shut.

"But—!" I began.

I was crying then. Tears streamed down my face. I thought about ringing the bell again, but I knew it would do no good. The bitch wouldn't let me see Den.

So I went home. I was shaking and crying and I felt sick inside.

I went up to my room and lay on the bed and sobbed my eyes out.

One hour later, my mobile rang.

I cried out and jumped off the bed. I grabbed my phone and shouted, "Yes? Is that you, Den?"

It wasn't Den. It was Kate. "Hi, Trish," she said.

"What do you want?" I asked.

"Just calling to see how you are," she said sweetly.

"What do you mean?" I asked.

"Well, me and Gaz wanted to know how things were between you and Denis?"

I felt sick. "How do you know?" I shouted at her. "What have you said to him?"

She hung up on me. I tried to ring her back, but she'd turned off her mobile.

I sat on the edge of the bed. My hands were shaking and I felt like I was going to be sick. I called Den's house again on my mobile. "Please, please pick the phone up, Den! Please!"

"Yes?" It was his mum again.

"Please, I need to speak to Den! It's important! Please let me speak to him!"

His mum said, "I don't think that's a good idea just now."

I heard another voice. It was Den. He was talking to his mum. He was saying, "I'm OK now. I'll talk to her."

My heart nearly burst. "Den!" I shouted. "What's happening?"

Den said, "As if you don't know! How could you, Trish? How could you be so cruel?"

I began to cry even more. "What?" I yelled. "What have I done!"

He said, "You never really liked me, did you? It was just a game to you. I was the dork and you were the stuck up bitch."

"Den, I love you!"

"I thought you *did* love me, Trish. I couldn't believe my luck when you said you wanted to go out with me. And all the times ... all the times we had together." He was crying now too, sobbing. "We were so happy. And then you went and did that!"

"Did what?" I yelled at him.

"Don't deny it, Trish. I know it was you. I found one of your school books there."

"I don't understand!" I said. "Where? Where did you find my book?"

"Under the oak tree. Next to the smashed eggs and the smashed nest. You must have dropped your book when you were destroying the kite's nest."

"Den," I said, "I swear, it wasn't me. I wouldn't do a thing like that! I haven't touched that nest!"

"You've been playing a game all along. You made me think you felt something for me. And all the time you just wanted to hurt me." He was crying so much that he couldn't go on.

The line went dead.

I tried to ring him again, but he didn't pick up the phone.

I curled into a ball and sat in the corner of my room. I cried until my throat was sore.

I knew what had happened. I worked it all out.

Kate and Gaz were going out – and the other day Gaz had said that he knew how to hurt both me and Den ...

Last week I'd told Kate about the red kite's nest in the big oak tree. I'd told her that I was going to smash it ... And then the other day, she'd been in my locker. She must have taken one of my school books.

Then she and Gaz had gone to the woods. They'd found the oak tree and the ladder, and destroyed the red kite's nest. Then they had left my book next to the smashed eggs.

So when Den found the book, he thought that I'd smashed the nest.

Gaz was right. He did know how to hurt both me and Den ... He'd done more than just hurt me, though, and smash the nest. He'd destroyed me.

I loved Den so much. I thought about the pain he was in. That made me cry even more.

That night I didn't sleep at all.

****

On Saturday morning I went round to Den's house, but he didn't come to the door. I rang him about 50 times, but he didn't answer.

On Monday morning I ran over to him in the school yard. I begged him to listen to me. I told him that Kate had done it, that she'd taken my book and left it under the tree ... But Den just looked at me as if he hated me. Then he walked away.

I saw Kate and Gaz were watching me.

They saw me staring at them, and they laughed.

Chapter 10

The Pain Inside

And that's the end of the story.

Every time I saw Den, I tried to tell him the truth. But of course he didn't believe me.

I still love Den. I still think about him all the time. I remember all the good times we had together, and I feel sick without him.

I look in my bedroom mirror, and what do I see?

I see a girl who looks beautiful. She's in smart clothes, she's got great hair and fantastic make-up ... But I remember what Den said. I know how I look on the outside doesn't really matter.

Because on the inside I feel so bad.

Barrington Stoke would like to thank all its readers for commenting on the manuscript before publication and in particular:

Sarah-Frances Bateson

Leanne Callaghan

Catriona Campbell

Robert Crowhurst

Jonny Druce

Luke Gale

Jamie Gill

Liz Hutton

Mrs S Kiel

F. Lawton

Mrs. J Lewis

Mrs June McCleave

Tam McKeever

Kimberly Morrison

Siobhan Smith

Sue Tomlinson

Jamie Underwood

Ainsley Webster

Become a Consultant!

Would you like to give us feedback on our titles before they are published? Contact us at the email address below – we'd love to hear from you!

info@barringtonstoke.co.uk
www.barringtonstoke.co.uk